My Brother, the Knight

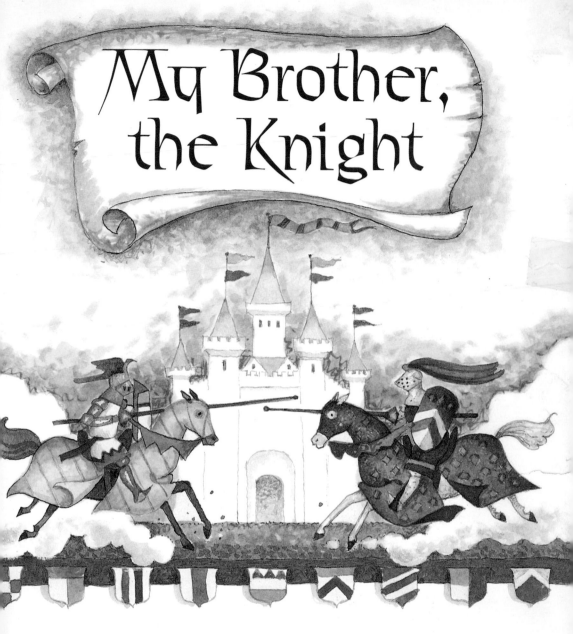

by Laura Driscoll
illustrated by Jerry Smath

The Kane Press
New York

To Larry S. Fasman, D.D.S. who lives on the biting edge.—J. S.

Acknowledgement: Our thanks to Linda Honan, M. Phil. (Medieval Studies, Yale), Manager, K–12 Academic Outreach, University of Massachusetts Amherst, for helping us make this book as accurate as possible.

Text copyright © 2004 by The Kane Press. Illustrations copyright © 2004 by Jerry Smath.

Library of Congress Cataloging-in-Publication Data

Driscoll, Laura.
  My brother, the knight / by Laura Driscoll ; illustrated by Jerry Smath.
      p. cm. — (Social Studies connects)
“History - grades: 1–3.”
Summary: Annoyed at his brother Colin’s obsession with knights, Jared challenges his younger brother to live one full week as if it were the Middle Ages.
  ISBN 1-57565-140-8 (pbk. : alk. paper)
  [1. Brothers—Fiction. 2. Knights and knighthood—Fiction. 3. Civilization, Medieval—Fiction.] I. Smath, Jerry, ill. II. Title. III. Series.
  PZ7.D79My 2004
  [Fic]—dc22
                                                        2003024178

10 9 8 7 6 5 4 3 2 1

First published in the United States of America in 2004 by The Kane Press.
Printed in Hong Kong.

Social Studies Connects is a trademark of The Kane Press.

Book Design/Art Direction: Edward Miller

www.kanepress.com

"*Ta da!*" said my brother, Colin. He held up the knight's shield he had just made.

"Look, Jared!" he said. "Or, as a knight would say, *behold!*"

I rolled my eyes. There was no way around it. Colin had gone nuts—nuts for knights.

It all started when Colin's class did a unit on knights and the Middle Ages. Ever since, all he talked about was knights, knights, and more knights.

WOW!

The knights that Colin learned about lived in Europe between the years 1050 and 1300. This was during a time called the Middle Ages. There were knights in other parts of the world, too.

Ancient times

Middle Ages

Modern times

The Middle Ages came between ancient times and more modern times. The Middle Ages are also called **medieval** times.

The Castle

Colin made his own armor and sword.

He made his own coat of arms.

A knight's main job was to be a soldier for his lord or king. A knight often wore a cloth coat over his armor. This was called his **coat of arms**. The design on it told people who the knight was. A knight did not write his name on his coat of arms, because back then very few people could read.

He made a horse. He even dressed our dog, Mack, to be his helper. "Every knight should have a page," Colin said.

A **page** helped his knight dress, served him food, and did other chores, too. Boys became pages when they were seven. As teenagers, they became **squires** and helped knights in battle.

"Knights are so cool!" said Colin. "I sure wish I lived in the Middle Ages."

"Are you kidding?" I said. I reminded Colin that in the Middle Ages there was no gas or electricity. There were no flush toilets. And there were no TVs, or computers, or video games!

"It's a good thing you didn't live back then,"
I said. "You wouldn't have lasted one week!"
"Oh, yeah?" said Colin.
"Yeah!" I said.
"Bedtime!" Mom called.

"I bet I *could* live like someone from the Middle Ages," Colin told me as he got into bed. "And I'll prove it, too! I'll live like a real knight for a whole week. If I can't, I'll do your chores all next week."

"It's a deal!" I said. "And if you *can* do it, I'll do *your* chores next week."

"Okay with you, Mom?" Colin asked.

"Okay," she said. "But I have some rules, Sir Colin. First, you still have to go to school. Second, you have to shower. Third, you have to eat what I cook. And you have to use the toilet—and flush! And if this gets out of hand, the bet is off. Got it?"

"Got it!" we said.

After a man became a knight, people called him "Sir." So a knight named George was called Sir George.

Sir Colin came down to breakfast on Monday in full armor. He sat down very close to me. Then he reached over to my plate and started to cut up my sausage.

"Hey! Do you mind?" I said.

Colin explained. "In the Middle Ages, two or more people shared a plate. Whoever was younger helped the other person eat."

Rich people had feasts with spiced meats, fish, stews, fruits, nuts, and fancy pastries. Poor people mostly ate bread, porridge, cheese, and vegetables like turnips. Nobody ate tomatoes or corn or potatoes, because back then they didn't grow in Europe.

Colin picked up a piece of sausage with his fingers. "Oh, yeah," he added. "And they ate most things with their hands." He held the sausage out to me. "Want some?"

I looked at Colin's greasy fingers. "I'm not hungry anymore."

Knights never used forks. Forks were not popular in Europe until long after the Middle Ages.

On Tuesday after school, Colin and I were
doing our homework. I looked up. "Colin—"

"Sir Colin," he corrected me.

I sighed. "All right. *Sir* Colin, may I borrow
your dictionary?"

"Umm . . ." Colin said, thinking it over. "No."

"No?" I said. "Why not?"

Colin told me that books were great treasures in the Middle Ages. "People hardly ever lent them out," he said. "But sometimes they rented them. So I guess I could *rent* my dictionary to you."

I put my head in my hands. "Never mind," I muttered.

There weren't many books in the Middle Ages because the printing press had not been invented yet. Each book was written out by hand. Often it took years to finish making just one!

17

Early Wednesday morning, I woke up to the
sound of Colin practicing his sword fighting.

"Take that!" he yelled. "And that!"

"What are you doing?" I said.

"It's the middle of the night!"

When knights weren't fighting real battles,
they were practicing their skills. They
competed against other knights in a sport
called jousting. In a joust, knights used
lances to try to knock each other off their
horses. Sometimes the winning knight would
get prizes, or the loser's horse, or armor.

Colin shrugged. "It's 4:00 A.M.," he said. "In
the Middle Ages, that's when most people got up.
They wanted to be ready to work as soon as it got
light. Remember? They didn't have electricity."

"Who cares?" I moaned. I pulled the covers
over my head.

On Thursday afternoon, Colin and I were playing checkers.

I wrinkled my nose. *Sniff, sniff.* "Do you smell that?" I asked Colin.

"Smell what?" he said.

I traced the smell to Colin's mouth.

"*Eeww!* It's your breath! Gross!"

Checkers, chess, backgammon, blind man's bluff, and dice were all popular games in the Middle Ages.

"Oh, that," said Colin. "I can't help it. Only rich people had toothbrushes in the Middle Ages."

"You mean you haven't brushed your teeth all week?" I asked.

Colin shook his head. He pulled a little twig out of his pocket. "Back then, most people just rubbed their teeth with one of these!"

People didn't visit their dentists for checkups, either. There weren't any real dentists in the Middle Ages. If someone had a bad toothache that wouldn't go away, there was just one cure. Pull out the tooth!

Friday was chore day. After school, Colin and I had to strip our beds, clean up our room, empty our wastebaskets, and bring our dirty laundry down to the basement.

But this Friday, Colin didn't stop at that. "How else may I serve you?" he asked Mom and Dad.

"Just use your knightly imagination," Mom said. Colin took all the trash out to the garage. He washed and dried all the dishes.

A knight was supposed to be brave, polite, and kind, especially to people who needed help. This way of behaving was called **chivalry**.

Colin brought the mail out to the mailbox. "Please deliver these, by order of my lord and lady!" he announced to the mail carrier.

Colin helped shoo away a squirrel that had gotten in through an attic window. "Be gone, furry scoundrel!" he called, waving his sword.

And he helped carry in the groceries.

"Why, thank you, Sir Colin," Mom said. "You've been extra helpful today."

"Just doing my duty, my fair lady and noble lord," said Colin. "As your knight, I serve and protect you. And you allow me to live on your land."

"Sounds great to me!" Dad exclaimed. "I could get used to this royal treatment."

A **lord** was a powerful man who let people live on his land and protected them from enemies. The people gave him something in return. Farmers gave some of the food that they grew. Knights fought for him. Craftspeople gave him their goods, or paid him taxes.

I heard what Dad said and I got really nervous.
What if Mom and Dad *did* get used to the royal
treatment? What if they expected it all the time? And
what if they expected *me* to be extra helpful, too?

I could just see it now. It could mean only one
thing—more chores.

I knew what I had to do. I had to end the bet—
and I had to do it now, before it was too late!

I pulled Colin into our room. "You have to stop acting like a knight," I said. "It's over. You won the bet."

"You're giving up?" Colin said. "Why?"

"If I give up now, I have to do your chores for one week," I said. "But if Mom and Dad get used to your royal treatment, we'll both end up doing extra chores *every* week—from now on!"

"But it's fun acting like a knight," Colin said. "I don't want to stop."

"Let's make a deal," I said. "You can act like a knight, but you can't do a zillion extra chores. And I'll still do your chores next week like I promised."

"And one more thing," said Colin.

"Okay! Okay!" I said. "Anything!"

At that Colin rushed out of the room. "Wait right here!" he ordered.

After what seemed like forever, Colin came
back. He handed me two big pieces of cardboard.
"All next week, you have to be my helper,"
Colin said. "Or as a knight would say, my *page*."

"But—but—you have a page! You have Mack—"
Then I stopped. There was no use arguing.
Colin was still nuts—nuts for knights.

I can role-play!

MAKING CONNECTIONS

Colin can role-play—and so can you! Role-playing is using your imagination to pretend that you are someone else. It's a great way to connect to the past! You can even ask your friends to join in!

Look Back
Colin is pretending that he lived in the Middle Ages. Look at pages 12 and 14. What is Colin doing? Why? What does he tell Jared on page 16? How else does Colin role-play?

Try This!
Take Colin's Challenge! Try role-playing with a friend. You can pretend to be anyone! Here are some suggestions.

Imagine that you are a Pilgrim, or a sailor with Columbus, or the leader of a wagon train going West. Or you can pretend to be an important person like Pocahontas, George Washington, or Martin Luther King, Jr.

What would your day be like? What would you wear? What would you do for fun? What chores might you have?

You may want to keep a journal or make a drawing of your day.

What other roles would you like to play?